Nineteen Hats, Ten Teacups, an Empty Birdcage &

THE ART OF LONGING

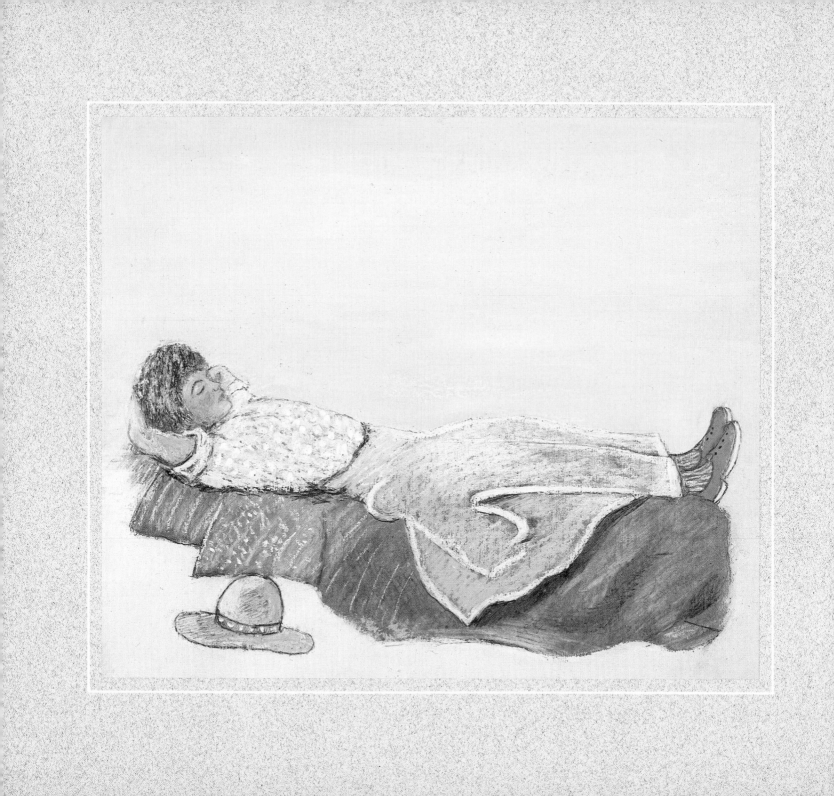

Nineteen Hats, Ten Teacups, an Empty Birdcage &

THE ART OF LONGING

by
Cooper Edens

GREEN TIGER PRESS
Published by Simon & Schuster
New York · London · Toronto · Sydney · Tokyo · Singapore

Longing, far more than it haunts you,

reminds you of your true name.

Longing that is with joy is complete longing.

When it is strong it calms us.

Longing is whatever one wishes.

It can tell you your life again.

Longing does not change anything.

It is the art of not knowing.

Longing is when we think our storm is the right size.

A little can be eternal.

Longing always visits one who is content.

It may be the gift no other gift provides.

Longing comes singly and leaves accompanied.

It can be happiness.

Longing is a word that means to put stars together:

the faith you instill, the faith it has instilled.

Longing is to be someone.

To be someone is solitude.

GREEN TIGER PRESS
Simon & Schuster Building
Rockefeller Center
1230 Avenue of the Americas
New York, New York 10020
Copyright © 1981 by Cooper Edens
All rights reserved including the right of reproduction
in whole or in part in any form.
GREEN TIGER PRESS is a trademark of Simon & Schuster.
Manufactured in the United States of America

10 9 8 7 6 5 4 3 2 1

(pbk.) 10 9 8 7 6 5

Library of Congress Cataloging-in-Publication Data
Edens, Cooper. Nineteen hats, ten teacups, an empty
birdcage & the art of longing / by Cooper Edens.
p.   cm.   Summary: Explores the notion that longing is a
meaningful and even desirable state of being.
[1. Contentment—Fiction.]   I. Title.   II. Title: Art of longing.
PZ7.E223Ni 1992 [Fic]—dc20 91-25277 CIP
ISBN 0-671-75592-7   ISBN 0-671-74968-4 (pbk.)